Books by Keely

THE UNCHARTED SERIES

The Land Uncharted

Uncharted Redemption

Uncharted Inheritance

Christmas with the Colburns

Uncharted Hope

Uncharted Journey

Uncharted Destiny

THE UNCHARTED BEGINNINGS SERIES

Aboard Providence

Above Rubies

All Things Beautiful

Christmas with the Colburns

Keely Brooke Keith

Edenbrooke
Press

Christmas with the Colburns

Copyright 2015 Keely Brooke Keith

Cover designed by Najla Qamber Designs
Edited by Dena Pruitt
Interior design by Edenbrooke Press
Author photo courtesy of Frank Auer

Printed in the United States of America

ISBN: 9781092603867

For Annalise

I treasure our friendship

Chapter One

Lydia Bradshaw refused to allow the Colburn house to go undecorated at Christmastime. Weaving among the bartering villagers at the open-air market, she anchored baby Andrew on her hip and scanned the traders' booths for tinsel, ribbon, garland—anything that might make her family's home look like it did when her mother was alive. Surely one of the traders or artisans had something left, even this late in December.

"I should have started making decorations weeks ago," she muttered to the baby, as if an eleven-month-old cared, "but with a medical practice, a house to manage, and a great-aunt to care for, it seems my favorite holiday has sneaked up on me like a cat on a mouse." She smiled down at Andrew as he sucked on his fingers. "Come to think of it, if our barn cats did their job and killed mice, my box of decorations from last Christmas wouldn't have been turned into a reeking, chewed-up nest."

Determined to make her and Connor's first Christmas with the baby a celebration to remember, Lydia dodged the carpet trader, avoided the hat-maker's boy, who was trying to demonstrate hairpins on unsuspecting customers—someone really should stop him—and turned before the gossipy wool spinner noticed her. As she passed the produce booth, tin cylinders with colorful labels caught her eye. Her skirt swirled as she turned on her boot heel. "Are these canned cherries already pitted?" she asked the young man working at the back of the booth.

He didn't respond and continued sprinkling sugar on a tray of freshly roasted nuts. That's where the luscious smell was coming from. Lydia cleared her throat and tried again. "Excuse me?"

The veteran produce trader stepped out from behind his wagon where he was unloading a crate of lemons. He yelled at his new worker, "It's your job to help the customers."

The young man snapped his attention to Lydia and hurried to the front of the booth. "Sorry. Yes, ma'am, canned pitted cherries from Riverside." He straightened his straw hat and grinned, revealing a broken bicuspid and swollen gums. "How many cans would you like?"

"Two please. No wait..." She mentally calculated the number of family members who would be coming for Christmas dinner this year. Fifteen... seventeen if Everett Foster and his mother, Roseanna, accepted her invitation. It would be the biggest crowd yet. She would have to double her mother's cherry salad recipe. "Four cans, please."

"Yes, ma'am." He removed the cans from his display. "What would you like to trade?"

"She's the village physician," the veteran trader interrupted, scowling at the young man. "This is Dr. Lydia Bradshaw, formerly Dr. Lydia

Colburn. You don't charge a doctor for cherries."

"It's quite all right." She looked at the young man. "How about four cans of cherries and I'll take care of that infected tooth for you?"

His cheeks reddened and he covered his mouth with his dirty fingers. "That sounds painful."

"I have medicine that will remove the pain, and once the tooth is out, you will feel much better."

"Thank you, ma'am. I accept your trade." He picked up the cans. "I'll just carry these to your wagon."

"I walked here." She shifted the baby to the other hip. "When the market closes this afternoon, come by my office. I live at the Colburn house—the two-story brick home near the south entrance of the village. The medical cottage is next door. Try the cottage first and if there's no answer, go to the back door of the house. And bring the cherries with you."

He nodded and spoke through barely parted lips, trying not to reveal his broken tooth again. "Thank you, Doctor. I'll be much obliged for your help."

As she resumed her search for decorating materials, Lydia spotted her father, John Colburn, the village overseer, on the chapel steps. The morning light made his trimmed beard appear grayer than usual. Though in his element, leaning against the iron railing, reciprocating greetings with happy couples as they passed, he also seemed lonely. Even after thirteen years, Lydia still missed her mother every day. Her father must miss her even more. He never spoke of his sorrow, but when no one else was looking—especially at Christmastime—Lydia saw the sadness in his eyes.

A cool breeze blew in from the nearby ocean and kept the air moving through the crowded village market. Someone stopped behind Lydia and rubbed Andrew's head. The baby let out a half-giggle half-squeal. Lydia smiled as she turned to Mandy. "He only makes that noise when he sees you."

"That's because I'm his favorite aunt." Mandy batted her eyelashes at the baby as she flipped her blanket of auburn curls over her shoulder and reached for him. She settled Andrew on the side of her pregnant belly. "And how is my little nephew this fine morning?"

Andrew responded with a slobbery giggle and rubbed a wet hand across her baby bump. Mandy laughed. "That's right! Your cousin is in there. You will get to meet him soon."

"Or her," Lydia interjected.

"Don't let Levi hear you say that," Mandy chortled. The noise sounded cute coming from her, but Lydia would sound like a horse if she did it. "He insists his firstborn will be a boy."

"Don't worry about Levi. My brother will be a proud father no matter what. To think, by next Christmas you will have your own little one crawling around the house." Lydia glanced across the market and remembered her purpose. "Have you seen Christmas decorations at any of the booths today? My decorations from last year are ruined. This is Andrew's first Christmas and it might be Aunt Isabella's last, so I want to make it special for everyone."

"No, I haven't." Mandy lowered her perfect chin. "Actually, I need to talk to you about that."

"About what?"

"Levi and I are going to celebrate Christmas at my mother's this year."

The news kicked Lydia in the gut, but she did her best not to show it. "Oh."

"It's just that this is our first year without Father, and I think it will help Mother if Levi and I spend the day with her and Everett."

"I invited your mother and Everett to our house too."

"Yes, I know, and it was kind of you, but Levi is eager to start our own traditions, and we think it will be best for our family if we go to

Mother's. She is thrilled with the idea. And Everett and Bethany will probably be married soon, and then Bethany will live out there too, so it really makes sense that we start that tradition now."

"Bethany is spending Christmas with Everett at your mother's also?"

"Well, she will be a Foster soon."

Lydia wanted her baby back. She held out her hands to Andrew. "I understand," she said, though she didn't understand at all. The Colburns always spent Christmas at the Colburn house. Her brother had married Mandy Foster, making her a Colburn, and Bethany wasn't married to Everett Foster yet, so she was still a Colburn. It would make more sense if Roseanna Foster and Everett came to them, not the other way around.

Mandy's empty hands covered her belly. Seven months pregnant and the tiny woman still wore the same dresses she had worn last year. She gave Lydia a sympathetic grin. "I'm sorry to disappoint you. It's better for us this way, and maybe it will be easier on you, less work and all that. And you have Connor and the baby with you at your father's house, so you will be with people you love. Isn't that what makes Christmas special?"

"Yes, I suppose."

Mandy glanced down at her belly. "We're all starting families, so this is the perfect time to start our own holiday traditions."

"I'm sure you're right." Lydia looked away. Wheels squeaked loudly as a man pushed a cart across the cobblestone street. Villagers shouted cheerful greetings to one another. The crowded market started to irritate her. She couldn't find decorations anyway. "I'm going home. Have you seen Connor?"

"He's at the messenger's booth." Mandy frowned. "You are upset, aren't you?"

"No." Lydia pressed her lips together. "I'm not."

"Yes, you are."

"All right, I am, but I'll get over it. I have my own family to focus on this Christmas. Besides, Adeline and Maggie and their families always come to Good Springs for the day, so the Colburn house will still feel full," she said as she cuddled Andrew close and started for the messenger's booth. "I have to go."

Mandy blew a kiss to the baby. "Merry Christmas."

"You too," Lydia called over her shoulder as she hurried away. She squeezed through the bartering villagers toward her husband.

Despite the flurry of activity around him, Connor stood near the messenger's booth like an immoveable pillar in the midst of whitewater rapids. He laughed at whatever joke the messenger told and easily focused on their conversation until his eyes met Lydia's. He held a finger up to the messenger and parted the crowd for Lydia.

Ignoring the hubbub, Connor grinned at her. "That never gets old."

"What doesn't?"

"Seeing you walk toward me." He bent down and kissed her as if he had just come home from war. The baby squeezed a drool-covered hand between their faces. When Connor released her, his expression bespoke a mixture of affection and arrogance. On him, it was charming.

He passed a hand over the baby's head, still gazing at Lydia. "Did you find what you needed to make your decorations?"

She shook her head. "It doesn't matter."

Connor's brow furrowed and his brown eyes filled with compassion. "Of course it does. You were really looking forward to this Christmas. What happened?"

She couldn't hide anything from him. "Five of the people I was counting on won't be there." She wanted to add that the news had crushed her spirit and might have ruined Christmas, possibly forever. She swallowed the complaint to keep it from passing between her lips, just like her mother had always instructed. "Roseanna is making Christmas dinner for Levi and Mandy and Everett and Bethany."

Connor put his hand on her shoulder. "Your younger siblings have the right to make their own plans. That's what happens when people grow up. Hey, you still have Andrew and me, your dad, and Isabella, plus your two elder sisters are coming with their families." He caressed her arm. When she didn't muster a smile, he continued trying to cheer her up. "What if I go into the forest and find a bunch of pine twigs and wind them together to make you some garland?"

He was kind to offer, but she had seen his attempts at crafts. The image made her chuckle. "No, that's not necessary." She readjusted the baby and pointed to Connor's fistful of letters. "Did the messenger have anything for me?"

He flipped through the envelopes and drew one out. "You got a letter from one of your sisters in Woodland."

"Splendid! Is it from Adeline or Maggie?"

Connor shrugged. "I can't tell their writing apart."

Lydia took the envelope and read it. An extra flourish adorned the L in Lydia. "It's from Adeline. She's probably letting me know what time they plan to arrive on Christmas." Her excitement grew as she unfolded the letter. "Maybe they'll come a day early and stay the night on Christmas Eve. Wouldn't that be lovely?"

"Uh huh," Connor hummed his answer as he opened one of his letters.

Lydia read Adeline's letter twice. It was only three sentences, so it didn't take long. Her cheeks grew hot and pressure built behind her eyes. She would not cry over this, and certainly not in public. She drew a long steadying breath and looked up at Connor. "They aren't coming."

Chapter Two

Clouds dimmed the afternoon sunlight, darkening Lydia's medical office, so she moved an oil lantern closer to the patient cot for more light. She gripped her surgical pliers with one hand and Nicholas Vestal's mud-caked foot with the other. As she pulled the rusty nail out of his heel, he howled so loudly she wished she had given him a rag to bite.

Baby Andrew laughingly mimicked Nicholas's cry and crawled across the medical office floor. Nicholas didn't seem to mind the baby, and Lydia was thankful. Connor always said not to imagine what others might think of her, but she was the first female doctor in the village of Good Springs and didn't want her hard-earned respect diminished.

"It's a good thing it was a short nail, Nicholas." She dropped the pliers and nail into a porcelain bowl on the counter beside the patient cot and pressed a piece of gauze against the bleeding puncture wound. "But it was rusted. Where did you step on it?"

"Behind the barn." His wooly sideburns puffed as he grimaced. "I was mending a gate."

"At the Foster farm? You work barefoot?"

"My boots had water in them. I had them drying in the sun."

"Why didn't you go and get another pair?"

"When? While the sheep were wandering down the road?" Nicholas drew his head back and glowered as though he'd sucked on a lemon. He was handsome in a rugged shepherd kind of way when he wasn't stretching his face into exaggerated expressions. "I'm working with Everett to earn my own flock. I'll owe more sheep than I earn if I can't keep the gates closed."

"I understand." She inspected the hole in the bottom of his foot. It needed to be flushed out. "Still, it would be best if you wore shoes while out-of-doors."

Nicholas narrowed his eyes as he reclined on the cot. "You sound like my aunt."

"I'm not. I'm the doctor. Hold your foot over this pan," she said as she poured clean water into the wound. The cool water mixed with blood and dirt as it dripped into the pan. "It makes no difference to me which one of us you listen to. Please wear shoes while you're working."

As she pressed clean gauze against Nicholas's punctured foot, baby Andrew crawled to her desk. He grabbed a drawer handle to pull himself up. The drawer slid open and popped the baby in the forehead. He fixed his brown eyes on Lydia, sucked in a breath, and wailed with such force even Nicholas flinched.

Lydia put Nicholas's hand over the gauze. "Hold this firmly over the wound," she said as she left her patient and scooped the baby from the floor. Andrew's forehead was fine, but he continued crying. A yawn interrupted his sobs, and his cry changed tone.

She held the baby as she returned to Nicholas and checked the gauze. "The bleeding stopped." She kissed Andrew's forehead as she reached for a jar of gray leaf ointment. He wasn't going to stop crying, and she had work to do.

She shifted the whimpering baby and used her free hand to open the jar. The gray leaf medicine's potent aroma filled the room with its sharp minty scent. Still holding the baby, she slathered a generous dollop of the medicinal salve on Nicholas's wounded foot. She closed the lid on the glass jar and held it out to him. "The gray leaf medicine in this should remove the pain within minutes. Take the rest of it home with you… or back to the Fosters' farm."

"I'm still living in the shepherd's cabin there."

"Right, well, use the ointment on the wound twice a day to ward off infection."

He nodded and then pointed at the crying baby. "He's got Connor's coloring."

"And Connor's need for adventure." Lydia rubbed Andrew's back as she stepped to the cabinet for bandaging material. She glanced at

Nicholas and tried to think of something to say to distract from the crying baby. "Do you have any special plans for Christmas?"

He shrugged. "I don't know if you'd call my plans special, but my aunt usually makes a big roast for dinner on Christmas Day. My family never had elaborate traditions like some people. My grandfather always said it was better not to have traditions than to be disappointed when they ended."

Lydia thought of her family's traditions and her disappointment with the coming holiday. "Our traditions changed when my mother died years ago. I've tried my best to keep some of the traditions alive, but it seems I'm the only one who cares anymore. Perhaps your grandfather was right—"

After one short knock, the office door opened a few inches. Bethany stuck her head inside. "Lydia, Aunt Isabella needs you."

Lydia crossed the medical office with three quick strides—still holding the baby—and met her younger sister at the door. "I'm with a patient. What does she need?"

Bethany fidgeted with the delicate silver bracelet at her wrist. "She asked for you. Oh, hello Nicholas. I wondered why Everett's wagon was parked out front."

Nicholas smiled apologetically. "Everett drove me here to see the doctor. It was just a nail in my foot, but he insisted. He's in the barn now."

"In the barn?" Bethany's countenance lit at the mention of Everett's presence. "I'll go see him."

"Wait." Lydia stopped her love-struck sister. "Can you help Isabella first, please?"

Bethany shook her head. "I tried. She doesn't need any help. She just wants you to sit with her."

"Tell her I will be back in the house in few minutes," Lydia raised her voice over Andrew's cries. "I'm almost done here."

Bethany touched the baby's arm. "What's wrong with Andrew?"

"He hit his head."

"Is he all right?"

"He's fine. It's past his naptime."

Bethany pointed at his back. "He has blood on his shirt."

Lydia checked the baby and saw a smear of her patient's blood. It was on her hand too. "I was in the middle of cleaning a wound when Andrew needed me."

Bethany reached for the baby. "I'll take him in the house with me."

"What about going to see Everett?"

"You need me more," she said, and then she looked at Nicholas. "Do tell Everett to come say hello before you leave."

Nicholas nodded. "I will."

Lydia kissed the baby then watched Bethany carry him away. "Thank you. Connor should be home from teaching school soon." She closed the door, washed her hands, and unwrapped the muslin material to cut a length for a bandage.

Nicholas raised himself to his elbows. "Everett told me about your aunt. She sounds like an interesting person. I wish I'd known her before she lost her faculties. Do you think her health will improve?"

"No. She's seventy-eight, blind, and has been bedridden for months. Her heart is still strong, but she doesn't know who anyone is anymore except..."

"Except you?"

"Except me. It's thoughtful of you to ask about her." Lydia wrapped the bandage around Nicholas's foot. "How does that feel?"

"Much better. Thank you." He wiggled his toes then stood. "You were right about the gray leaf ointment. I can't feel the pain at all now."

"Remember to use the rest of it like I told you."

He limped to the door, keeping the heel of his bandaged foot off the floor. "It doesn't hurt, but

I probably shouldn't press my heel to the ground, should I?"

"No. And please wear shoes while you're working from now on."

A grin spread to his sideburns. "Yes, of course." He stopped at the door. After a moment, pensiveness filled his eyes. "I must say I'm impressed with you. Not many women could manage a household and a baby and an ailing relative and keep working as the village's physician. You seem to do it all with grace to spare."

"That's a very kind thing to say." Lydia followed him to the door and pointed at his foot. "You're welcome to wait here and I'll go tell Everett to take you home."

"No, thank you. I can handle it." He smiled as he left the medical cottage. "Thank you, Doctor Bradshaw."

Chapter Three

Morning light flooded the kitchen as Lydia opened the back door of the Colburn house. Heat from the wood-burning oven and the scent of freshly baked cinnamon rolls warmed the wide room. She checked the oatmeal on the stove. Breakfast was ready, Bethany had taken juice and a boiled egg to Aunt Isabella, and Connor was dressing Andrew. The house was peaceful and tidy, but inside Lydia felt like a mess. She peeked into the stocked pantry and sighed. Less than a week until Christmas, but since her guest list had shrunk from seventeen to five, she had lost her motivation to begin preparations.

Connor carried Andrew into the kitchen. He kissed Lydia then sat at the table. Andrew giggled as his father bounced him on his knee. They should be reason enough to cook a big

Christmas dinner. If her siblings were starting their own traditions, maybe she should too.

She spooned oatmeal into Andrew's tiny bowl and stirred it. "Ready for some breakfast?"

Connor reached for the little bowl. "Here, I'll feed him."

"Are you sure? You need to leave soon."

"I have time. Today's the last day of school. All I have to do is give the final exam and grade the tests when the students are done. This year my class is a smart group of kids. They'll be finished by lunch."

Lydia smiled as she reached for the serving tongs. "They have a good teacher." She pulled two hot cinnamon rolls from the steaming pan and put one on her plate and one on Connor's then sat beside him.

Andrew wiggled and grabbed for the spoon as Connor blew on the oatmeal. "Hang on a second, pal. It's too hot for you."

John walked into the kitchen, running his fingers through his graying hair. "Good morning," he said as he stretched his suspenders over his shoulders. "Today will be another fine day. Not a cloud in the sky."

Lydia glanced at him as she picked up her fork. "Good morning, Father."

John lifted the coffee pot from the stove and carried it to the table. He offered Connor a refill then sat at the head of the table. Creases lined the corners of his crystal blue eyes as he flashed the baby a grin. "How is my grandson this morning?"

Andrew squealed, and oatmeal dribbled to his chin. Connor wiped it with the edge of the spoon and re-fed it to the baby. "He's eating like a champ."

"Excellent. Grow up big and strong like your father." John handed Connor a napkin. "Lydia, what are your plans for the day?"

Before she could answer, Bethany shuffled in from the parlor, holding a tray of untouched food. "I couldn't get Aunt Isabella to wake up." She set the tray on the counter and looked at Lydia. "Maybe you should check on her."

John stood so quickly his wooden chair made a sharp screech on the floor. Lydia accidentally swallowed a bite of cinnamon roll without chewing it. The painful lump made her cough as she rose to leave the table.

John passed behind her chair. "Finish your breakfast. I will go check Isabella."

Bethany sank into the chair across from Lydia. She curled her long legs into her chest and whispered, "Do you think Aunt Isabella is—"

"Shh!" Connor silenced Bethany as he tried to listen. Even the baby held perfectly still until two muffled voices came from the back bedroom.

John returned a moment later. "She was sleeping."

Bethany sighed and released her legs. "Oh, thank God. When I was trying to wake her, I didn't consider that she might be dead."

John laid his napkin in his lap. "Be prepared. Her time is coming soon."

"Father, that's a horrible thing to say!"

He selected a cinnamon roll from the pan and arched an eyebrow at Bethany. "It is the truth. She has not been out of bed for days. You must prepare yourself so that you do not go into shock, should you be the one to discover she has passed."

Bethany frowned. "I don't want to think about it." She stood and carried her empty juice glass to the sink. "I promised Mrs. Vestal I'd take care of all the orders at the pottery yard today. I have to go to work."

John cut a piece of cinnamon roll with his fork and swirled it in the white icing on his plate. "Before you leave," he said as he pointed to a pail by the pantry, "please go milk Greta."

Bethany picked up the bucket. "Fine. But who is going to milk the cow after I get married and move out? Baby Andrew?"

Connor chuckled as he scraped the last of the oatmeal from Andrew's bowl and fed it to the baby. "He'll be old enough to handle the chore by then—the way you and Everett are dragging your feet to the altar."

"Very funny." Bethany strode out the back door.

John finished his breakfast and held his hands out to take the baby. "Come see your grandfather, Andrew." He looked at Connor. "Last day of school?"

"Yes, sir."

"Have you decided what you will do during the break?"

"You mean about training to be the next overseer?" When John nodded, Connor pushed his plate of uneaten breakfast away. "I think we should get the approval of the other villages' overseers first. If they don't think I should be the next overseer of Good Springs, then I don't even have a decision to make."

John sipped from his coffee mug. The baby took a playful swipe at the cup. John didn't flinch. He placed it on the table out of Andrew's reach. "Since the role of village overseer is normally passed from father to son, it might seem like a radical change to some people— my training a man who is my son-in-law and not my son—but the overseers of the other villages understand our situation. It is no secret that Levi has never felt called to be the next overseer of Good Springs. The elders have prayed for years that God would send the right man for the position after me. I believe you are that man."

"I'm open to the possibility, but there are parts of the job I'm not ready for."

"You are a natural leader." John patted the baby's back. "Most people in the village recognize your authority. And we already know you are a good teacher."

Connor leaned forward. "I have no problem settling disputes, officiating weddings, and having the final say in village business; it's the weightier responsibility of pastoring the church that deserves more consideration." He pressed his hands together and stared at the peak of his fingers. "I have so much to learn."

Lydia listened to her father and husband as she began cleaning the kitchen. They rarely spoke about village business at the breakfast table, and she liked being allowed to listen. She pressed the wooden foot pedal beneath the sink, and water pumped in from the well.

John continued trying to convince Connor to accept his calling. "That is why we should begin your training during the summer months while you are free of your teaching duties. I am fifty-four years old. My father and grandfather both passed away before they were my age. I might live another thirty years and be able to continue working as overseer, or I might need a replacement next month. Since my son is not called to the position, I must find another man to train." John passed the baby back to Connor. "You are right to give this decision much prayer and consideration, but I have full confidence that you are the right man for the position. I want you to ride out to Woodland Monday morning and spend a few days with the overseer there. It is time to move the process forward."

Lydia dropped the metal tongs into the sink, and the sharp clink drew everyone's attention. "A few days? In Woodland? But Christmas is Thursday!"

Connor gave her a don't-worry-about-man-business look and patted the air. "I'll be back for Christmas, I promise."

John glanced between them. "I will let the two of you discuss it," he said as he walked out the back door. "But I will need your answer soon, Connor."

Lydia took the baby from Connor. "This will be Andrew's first Christmas, and already most of my family members have made other plans. You have to be here."

"I'll be here, but I really think you're making too much of this. I know you want all of your siblings to be here every Christmas for the rest of your life, but you have to let people do what's right for them. I think it's good that Levi and Mandy are going to spend the day with Roseanna and Everett at the Fosters' farm, since it's their first year without Samuel. And your sisters aren't being selfish. Their families are growing too, and the long wagon trip here is hard on the children." Connor shrugged and put his coffee mug in the sink. "Besides, the seasons are opposite here in the Land from what I grew up with in America, so it never feels like Christmas to me anyway. As a kid I felt sorry for people living on the Southern Hemisphere—warm Christmases and cold Julys—and now I'm one of you." He winked at her, but she didn't smile.

He spoke casually about the one holiday tradition that was important to her: having her whole family together on Christmas Day. It was her way of honoring her mother. How could she give that up?

She backed away from the sink. "Fine," she huffed as she carried the baby out of the room.

"Go spend the week in Woodland. My Christmas is ruined anyway!"

Chapter Four

Lydia pulled the hairpins from her chignon and dropped them into a glass votive atop her dresser. When she glanced into the mirror, her reflection reminded her more of her mother than of herself. She averted her eyes and picked up her hairbrush.

After a few slow strokes, she flipped her hair behind her back and waited for Connor to notice her new nightgown. Sitting on the other side of the bed, he stared into the wardrobe as he unbuttoned his shirt. He rarely went this long without looking at her.

She rubbed her bare arms, hoping to draw his attention to the gown's lack of sleeves. "Mandy has taken up sewing. She says it's nesting since she only has a few weeks until the baby comes, but her clothing designs are anything but matronly."

He removed his socks and dropped them on the floor.

She blew out the flame of the oil lamp on her bedside table and straightened the dainty silk bow on her gown's low-cut neckline. "So what do you think?"

"Hm?" He kept his back to her. The low light of his lamp defined his muscular build.

"About the nightgown Mandy made for me?"

He angled his chin toward her. "Nice."

"Connor? Are you mad about this morning?"

"No."

"Because I was just frustrated with my family. I'm sorry I took it out on you."

He lowered his head into his hands. "That's not it."

"What brought this on?" She moved across the bed and wanted to touch him, to wrap her arms around him, to pull him from whatever abyss his thoughts had dragged him into. But she waited. He would feel her near him and reach for her when he was ready. Whenever he was smothered by that dark silence, her insides twisted into aching knots. She put her hand to her stomach and asked God to give him peace.

Connor lifted his head but still did not look at her. His voice was low and gruff. "Don't do that."

"Don't do what?"

"Worry about me."

She removed her hand from her middle. "I was praying for you."

He let out a quick breath—the kind that would ordinarily prelude a chuckle—and cast his gaze to the ceiling. "I'm sorry. Yes, do that. Definitely do that."

She laid her cheek against the warm skin of his back. "What has happened?"

"Nothing." He rubbed his thumb along the lace strap at her shoulder. "This new?"

"It is." She touched the silk bow as she searched his face. His eyes were on her, but the darkness remained. His effort to hide his anxiety was valiant, but unnecessary. "Are you going to Woodland tomorrow?"

He raked his fingers through his hair, and it left black grooves like a plowed field. "I have to. I know you're worried about your holiday traditions, but your father is right: I need to make the decision whether or not I'll train to be the next overseer of Good Springs. I've put this off long enough."

"I didn't mean to make things harder on you."

Connor furrowed his brow. "You've never made things hard on me. You make my life complete. I love you and Andrew and this family and this village. I want to do the right thing for everyone."

She had grown used to the idea of her husband becoming the next leader of Good Springs someday, and she was beginning to like it. It meant they would live their lives in the Colburn house, but it also meant they would both have jobs that would frequently interrupt family time, including holidays. But if it were what he was called to do, she could deal with the inconveniences. "It's just bad timing, that's all."

"I don't want to leave you at Christmastime, especially while Isabella is near death and you're busy with the baby and work. And I know you're upset because the rest of your family is doing their own thing this year, but your dad will be here. This is his house, after all." He was smiling now. She could hear it in his voice. "I will try my best to be back by Christmas dinner. I have to do this and I need you to trust me. Okay?"

"All right."

"Good." He peeled the quilt back. "Now let's forget about it for tonight, please. At any moment a villager could bring a sick or wounded person to the medical office and ring the bell, and we won't have another quiet moment alone for days."

As Connor leaned onto the pillow beside her and pulled her close, the detestable darkness receded. The sweetness of being together in the quiet of the night took its place. As he traced a finger along her arm, she let out a contented sigh. She could not forget everything was changing, but she could put it aside long enough to enjoy their time together.

Something downstairs rattled the wall. Connor shifted in the bed and the quilt rustled. Beneath the sound, voices murmured outside. Before she could listen for it again, the bell on the wall rang.

She jumped out of bed and pinched the wire so the bell would stop ringing before it woke the whole house. This was the last thing she needed right now, but duty swallowed self-pity. She pulled a work dress over her fancy new nightgown.

Connor tossed the covers off and stood. He reached for his shirt. "I'll go out to the medical office with you."

"No, stay here. Remember, you have your work and I have mine. Besides, if Andrew wakes up, he'll need you. We can't expect Bethany to watch him all the time; she'll move out soon." She pointed at the bedside table. "Would you light my lamp for me, please?"

"Here, take mine."

She buttoned her dress. "No, I need mine."

"What you need is an assistant." He moved to her table, struck a match, and lit her lamp. As he carried it to her, he raised an eyebrow. "Ever thought about getting a nurse?"

"A what?"

"A nurse."

She laced her boots in case the person at the door needed her to ride out somewhere to help someone. "For Andrew?"

"No, in the medical office. One of the students graduating this year, Sophia Ashton, wants to train with you."

"Doctor Ashton's granddaughter?"

"Yeah. What do you think?"

"I can't think about it right now. I have to go." Lydia grabbed a hairpin from her dresser and reached for the door. "Don't wait up."

"Lydia?"

"Yes?"

"Please be careful."

Chapter Five

Lydia nestled Andrew into his crib for his afternoon nap, covering him with his favorite blanket. He promptly kicked it off and stuffed his foot into his mouth, then watched her to see if she would try to cover him again.

"I'm not falling for it, mister." She smiled at him and closed the nursery door behind her.

Exhausted from being awake with a patient all night, she was tempted to flop onto her bed and sleep too, but Isabella needed care. As she descended the stairs, Lydia picked up a bundle of dirty laundry she had left on the landing. It would get washed Monday no matter what. She dumped the laundry in the kitchen by the pantry, loaded a tray with Isabella's favorite afternoon snack, and took it to her great aunt's bedroom.

Isabella's door stood open and the heavy drapes were tied back, allowing the afternoon sun to light the room. Lydia raised her voice as she entered. "Aunt Isabella, it's me, Lydia. Would you like something to eat?" She set the tray on the doily-covered nightstand. "I brought you tea and shortbread cookies."

"Seventy-eight years I've lived in this room, and I've always kept the curtains closed in the afternoon." Her gravelly voice sounded painful. "I don't like how the sun heats the room when it hits the windows."

Lydia peeled back the quilts and touched her blind aunt's hand. "Your skin is cold. A little extra heat won't hurt you."

"I don't like sunshine coming in here," Isabella mumbled. "It'll shrink the rug."

"I need the light." Lydia reached for a vile of balm and dabbed it on Isabella's chapped lips. "Would you like some tea?"

"No, dear." Isabella pressed her lips together. "I need you to go to my wardrobe and get something."

"Of course. What do you need?"

"It's not for me, child. It's for you." Isabella lifted a crooked finger. "Inside, at the back of the top drawer, beneath the shawl. It's a family journal that was entrusted to my keeping. I should have given it to you long ago, but I always feared it would only sadden you."

Though she didn't expect to find anything in the drawer, Lydia stepped to the varnished wardrobe and opened its smooth doors. The scent of lavender wafted out as she followed her aunt's instructions. She drew out the shawl, and at the back of the drawer beneath a sachet of dried lavender was a pocket-sized notebook. Its thick paper cover was crisp, as if the notebook had hardly been touched, let alone written in. She opened the cover and there in her mother's handwriting it said: Private. If found, please return to Mrs. Hannah Colburn.

It couldn't be. Lydia's stomach tightened. Once desperate for her departed mother, she had asked her father if he had anything her mother had written. He had said her mother never kept a journal.

She flipped to the first page: I expected my eighteenth Christmas to be a lonesome holiday, missing my family and dreading the future, but one week with the Colburns of Good Springs changed my life forever.

It didn't read like a journal at all, but more of a personal narrative. Lydia clapped the notebook shut. "Who wrote this?"

"Your mother. She was having emotional difficulty after your birth. I suggested she write her account of the happiest time in her life, to help her overcome her sadness. After she wrote about falling in love with your father, she brought the journal to me and said she couldn't bear the thought of someone reading what she had written. She wanted to burn it. I convinced her to let me hide it." Isabella blew out a long breath. "And now I'll hide it with you."

Though the journal was small, it felt heavy in Lydia's hand. "Why me? I'm grateful, I really am, but shouldn't Father have it?"

Isabella closed her unseeing eyes and lay back against the pillow. "That is up to you, but since you are facing Christmas with sorrow, I think you should read it first."

"Did writing the story help Mother overcome her sadness?"

Isabella didn't answer. Her head lolled to the side.

"Aunt Isabella?" Lydia felt the pulse at her neck. It came in weak intermittent beats. She adjusted the pillows and raised the quilt to Isabella's emaciated shoulders. "Rest now. I'll be back to check on you in a little while."

She slipped the little journal into her dress pocket and left Isabella's room. With her two charges sleeping, Lydia took slow steps through the parlor and into the kitchen. She treasured the quiet of the house, and her only duty at present was to savor the silence. She sat in the wingback chair beside the stone hearth and propped her weary feet on the footstool.

The clock on the wall behind her clicked heavily, as it did every hour. She didn't need to look back to know the time. Two o'clock. Connor was at the chapel, studying theology with her father, and Bethany was working at the pottery yard, probably loading her work into the kiln.

For the moment, no one needed her, and it was a welcome relief. She let her head rest against the back of the chair. As she closed her eyes, a soft knock rattled the back door. She hurried out of the parlor and through the kitchen to answer the door, hoping neither the baby nor Isabella would be disturbed.

A young woman with chestnut hair swept up in a puffy bun raised a knuckle to tap again on the window of the back door. Lydia quickly pulled it open.

"So sorry to disturb you, Dr. Bradshaw," she said, smoothing the ribbing on her dress. "Mr.

Bradshaw told me to come to the back door if you didn't answer the door at the medical cottage."

"It's quite all right." Lydia gave the young woman a quick scan as she pulled the door closed behind her to limit the sound that bled through the house. "Are you ill?"

"Oh, no. Nothing like that," she smiled. "I'm Sophia Ashton. I'm in Mr. Bradshaw's class— was in his class. I just finished school yesterday and he told me to come talk to you about possibly training with you."

"Oh, yes. He mentioned it." Lydia shielded her eyes from the afternoon sun and instantly saw the Ashton family resemblance. "You have your grandmother's eyes."

"Thank you. She and Grandfather always spoke well of you." Sophia glanced at the closed kitchen door, as if awaiting an invitation.

"My baby is taking his nap at the moment, and my great aunt is not well. She is also resting."

Lydia pointed at the medical cottage. "Let's go into my office to talk."

"Okay," Sophia beamed. "That's one of Mr. Bradshaw's words. I'd never heard the word until I came to Good Springs, but all the students here say it. I rather like Mr. Bradshaw's expressions. It must be fascinating for you, being married to an outsider."

"At times." It was less fascinating when young women drooled over her husband, but she had gotten used to that long ago and had decided to consider it flattering.

The knob squeaked as she opened the door to the medical cottage. She slid her mother's journal into her desk drawer and motioned to the chair beside her desk. "Have a seat."

Sophia cast her gaze about the room. "I adore your cottage. I can't imagine having a space like this all to myself. It must have been lovely living out here all by yourself."

Lydia sat at her desk and glanced at the stairs that led to her old bedroom. "It was nice."

"And probably so quiet not having children around."

"Pardon?"

"Oh, not that your baby is loud." Sophia blushed. "I was thinking of my niece and nephew. They are twins—eighteen months old. They make quite a racket, screaming all day and waking each other up at night. I have to sleep in their room. Not that I mind."

"Aren't you living with your sister and her family in Doctor Ashton's old house?"

"That's right."

Lydia visualized the floor plan of her late mentor's home. "I thought it had three bedrooms."

"My sister and her husband keep separate bedrooms. She says that will ensure they don't have any more twins."

Lydia almost laughed. Instead, she raised her palm. "It's none of my business. Where are your parents?"

"Still in Woodland. My sister insisted I come to Good Springs to finish school, because everyone spoke highly of Mr. Bradshaw's teaching. I'm glad I did for that reason, but she really wanted me to come so I would mind her children for her."

"So now that you've finished school, why not return to Woodland?"

"I planned to, but…" Sophia touched the stone mortar and pestle Lydia kept on her desk. She traced the edge with her fingertip. "I've been reading my grandfather's journals, and I've become intrigued with the gray leaf medicine. It's my desire to assist you in your research. I want to learn more about the gray leaf and see what else it can do."

Lydia grinned. "Perhaps it can cure screaming toddlers."

"Perhaps." Sophia chuckled. "I know a medical apprenticeship takes years of study and training, and I'm not sure that I could be a doctor. All I know is that I want to help people and I want to study the gray leaf."

Lydia leaned her forearms against the desk. Some days her work was quiet, but with baby Andrew and having to care for Aunt Isabella, she didn't have time for the gray leaf research she longed to do. And then there were days when she was called to duty. She lived for those moments of rescue and medical intervention, sometimes saving a life. But often in the hours of patient observation afterward, she wished she had an assistant.

Sophia had the desire, intelligence, the Ashton lineage, and a healthy sense of humor. Perhaps this could work. "I'm only a few years into my career, so I don't consider myself ready to take on a medical apprentice. However, since you're interested in research, if you're also interested in learning patient care, I'd be willing to train you as an assistant."

"Oh, thank you, Dr. Bradshaw! You won't regret it!"

Lydia pointed to the stairs that led to the empty bedroom. "The job comes with housing." When Sophia clasped her hands excitedly, Lydia held up a finger. "But it also requires your being willing to watch my son when my duties demand my attention."

Sophia's pretty smile held steady. "I'd be happy to."

"Are you sure? Because I don't want you to feel like you're trading one set of babysitting duties for another. It wouldn't be often that you'd have to mind him—only when I have a patient and Connor isn't home."

"It would be my pleasure."

"Be sure to discuss it with your sister. She might not be happy about your leaving. I don't want any ill feelings, as if I'm taking her babysitter. I'm not. That would only be a small part of your duties. Your medical training would come first."

Sophia nodded enthusiastically. "I'll discuss it with her, but I'm sure she'll agree that it would be good for me to train for a profession."

"Great." Lydia stood from the desk and walked to the bannister. "Would you like to see your new room?"

Chapter Six

"Surely goodness and mercy shall follow me all the days of my life: and I will dwell in the house of the Lord forever." Lydia closed her Bible, believing Isabella had fallen asleep. Though the mid-morning light flooded her great-aunt's bedroom, it felt dark. With the heavy drapes tied back and the sash windows raised, fresh air flowed through the room as a salty-sweet breeze blew in from the ocean. It lifted the edge of a doily that topped the table by Isabella's rocking chair and knitting basket. She hadn't sat there to knit in months. Her knitting basket held a half-finished pink and blue blanket that was meant for Levi and Mandy's firstborn. The baby would come in another month or so, but Isabella would not finish the blanket.

"More," Isabella wheezed, her torso propped up by pillows.

Lydia nodded, even though Isabella wouldn't see her. She continued with the Twenty-fourth Psalm. "The earth is the Lord's and the fullness thereof." She glanced away from the page. Isabella's blind eyes were closed and her sallow face taut, but she was mouthing every word from memory as Lydia read. "...the world, and they that dwell therein."

Isabella stopped mouthing the words and Lydia paused her reading. Her great aunt took a deep breath and then went completely still. Lydia watched her chest, waiting for it to move with exhalation.

She counted the seconds in her head.

When thirty had passed, she slid her Bible onto Isabella's nightstand and reached for her aunt's hand. The instant Lydia touched her, Isabella sat straight up in bed. Her eyes opened wide and she smiled as if seeing a friend in front of her. Her lips twitched as though she were about to speak, but only a long breath hissed from her open mouth.

Lydia glanced at the wall opposite the bed. There was no one else in the room. They were alone. As she looked back at her aunt, Isabella closed her eyes and slumped onto the pillows.

Lydia moved swiftly out of professional reflex, as though she could catch this woman she loved and keep her another day—even another hour—but her time in this world had ended.

Isabella's body lay inert, her soul at peace in a new body with seeing eyes and dancing feet, but Lydia held on longer and harder than she intended. This was the woman who had filled some of the void after her mother died and the only person she had allowed herself to cry in front of. This was the friend whose support gave her the confidence to become the first female doctor in Good Springs and who encouraged her through every difficulty. This was the person who first told her Connor was a good man when others were suspicious of the outsider.

She wanted Isabella back for one more minute, one more verse, one more laugh, one more quiet conversation where her aunt would listen to her and reassure her and give her the kind of advice that had made Lydia the down-to-earth woman she was. Just once more. But she was gone.

"Thank you. I will never forget you." Lydia kissed Isabella's forehead and wept.

* * *

Lydia held Andrew close and wrapped her woolen shawl around them both as she stepped outside. The unseasonable chill in the air pricked her skin. At least she tried to tell herself it was the cool morning air that was making her skin crawl.

Dewy grass wet her ankles as she met Connor beside his horse. She didn't want him to go. "Do you have everything you need?"

He wiped his hands on his pants and then tousled Andrew's hair. "Yeah." He fastened a buckle on a saddlebag and looked at her with the half grin and unshakable confidence she had fallen in love with. Her heart skipped a beat as the pull that initially attracted her drew her once again. He was her husband, her lover, the father of her child, and he was riding out to another village when she needed him most.

Her voice lost its authority as she continued her half-wife, half-doctor orders. "I put a jar of ground gray leaves in your satchel, as well as a jar of ointment and—"

"I'll be fine, Doc."

"And a roll of bandaging material—"

He reached for her and drew her and the baby close. "Don't worry about me. I can take care of myself. I will miss you both, but I will be back on Christmas Day."

Her chin quivered and she tried to control it. She had held back her tears through Isabella's burial and the long night that followed, so she could hold them back a few more minutes. She managed a nod.

His dark eyes peered into hers. "Are you okay?"

"Of course." No matter how she tried, there was nothing she could hide from her husband. "I'm fine."

"No, you're not."

She didn't want his worry any more than he wanted hers. "Connor, I have a baby and a house to take care of, and Sophia is moving into the cottage tomorrow, so I'll have plenty to keep me occupied. She's excited to learn, and that gives me something to look forward to."

A playful smile broke his solemn expression. "Did you know your nose turns pink when you're trying not to cry?"

She straightened her posture. "I said I'm fine."

His seriousness returned. "You're not... but you will be." He stroked her arms and pressed his lips to her forehead. "I know you miss Isabella, and losing her will make you miss your mom too. You're a strong woman."

"I know."

"Do you?" He pulled back and locked her gaze with his. "This will be hard, but it's not going to break you."

"What about you? The other overseers in the Land might be grateful that Father has found his replacement in Good Springs, but they will not make this process easy on you."

"Don't worry about me. I can handle anything." His confidence was back to borderline cockiness, and she liked it.

She looked up at him. "I love you."

"I love you." He kissed her like it was their wedding day. "Miss me."

"I will."

Chapter Seven

Lydia emptied a basket of Andrew's toys on the parlor rug and sat the baby in the midst of them. As he began to play, she stared out the window at the empty road and let her eyes lose focus. Connor was gone. He would be back by Christmas dinner like he said—if he could help it. But it was a long day's ride to Woodland on horseback, and so many things could happen to him along the way. What if he fell from his horse or got sick or had a heart attack on the road and no one came by for hours—possibly days?

No, she shouldn't think like that.

Her heart could ache from mourning Isabella's death, and the big house could feel empty with her husband away, but she could not let her imagination frighten her with endless possibilities. Connor had told her not to worry about him, and that wasn't an arbitrary order but a directive meant to protect her peace. She needed a distraction.

She snapped her gaze from the road outside and sank her hand into her dress pocket. Her fingers traced the little journal Isabella had given her. She pulled it out of her pocket. It still smelled like lavender. Her aunt had said it told the story of her mother's happiest time. Lydia's father probably should have been given the journal first. If it were about him and his wife, he should decide who reads it. But at present, he was working in the barn and had no idea the pocket-sized notebook existed.

The house was quiet, save for Andrew's babbles as he inspected his wooden ABC blocks. Lydia lowered herself to the rug beside him and leaned her back against the divan. She opened the journal's cover. A tear blurred her vision as she read her mother's name, written by her mother's hand. The story begged to be read, so her fingers turned the page.

I expected my eighteenth Christmas to be a lonesome holiday, missing my family and dreading the future, but one week with the Colburns of Good Springs changed my life forever.

The Monday after my eighteenth birthday, my parents told me I had an hour to pack my things. At first I thought Father was jesting, but one look at Mother's pink nose and quivering chin and I knew this was serious.

Mother's eyes implored me to understand as she explained. "Your grandmother needs a caretaker, and I'm her only child. I'm also the heir to her property in Northpoint. The elders there have decided I can only claim the inheritance if your father and I move there immediately and take care of her. It's right for us to go back to Northpoint."

"Go back? But I was born here. The village of Good Springs is my home." I staggered back and gripped the quilt rack to steady myself. "You want me to move to Northpoint with you? Today?"

Father carried an old trunk into my room and plunked it down at the foot of my bed. "We'd hoped you would find a husband before you finished school, but you didn't. You're still my responsibility, and you can't stay here alone."

"I wouldn't be alone. Charles is staying here, isn't he?"

"Yes, he is. This farm is your brother's now." The trunk's iron hasp creaked as Father opened the lid. "We are hopeful that you will find a husband in Northpoint."

I glared into the splintery trunk. "I don't want to leave Good Springs. Not like this."

My father sighed. "The house in Northpoint is much bigger. You'll see. And since your brother gets this property, if you come with us, you'll inherit the Northpoint property one day."

"It has a beautiful orchard," Mother chimed in. "You'll love it there."

"Why can't I stay here with Charles?"

Mother gave Father a look, and he answered, "Since your brother is married now, he and his wife need their privacy."

"She hates me doesn't she?"

Mother raised a palm. "She does not hate you. This is best for all of us. You can either go with us to Northpoint or you can accept Cousin Virginia's offer. In her last letter she said she would love to have you live with them in Riverside. She was sure she could find you a husband in her village. You can help her with the children until you're married."

"Cousin Virginia and her husband have nine children. Of course they're eager for live-in help." I sat on the bed and scooted away from the stinky trunk. "I don't want to move to Riverside either."

"But you love children. You've always said you want a big family someday."

"Of my own."

"It's that or come to Northpoint with your father and me. We are taking the wagon, so if you go to Riverside, you'll have to ride with the next trader who is going west." Mother sat beside me and the mattress sagged. "I'm sorry this is sudden, but we just got the message today. We stopped at the Colburns' house after we heard the news and told the overseer and his wife our plans. Mrs. Colburn said if you decide to go to Riverside, you are welcome to stay with them until the traders go through the village on Saturday."

All I wanted in life was to marry a kind and godly man and fill a home with children. And even though I didn't have any prospects, I always imagined it would be here in Good Springs. Riverside and Northpoint were both so far away—several days by wagon—and both options seemed so final.

If I went to Northpoint, I would be with my parents and someday inherit my grandmother's property, but I would have to leave immediately. If I went to Riverside, I would probably end up a spinster nanny for my cousin's children, but at least I would have a few days more in Good Springs to tell my friends goodbye.

I started packing. "Fine. I'll go to Cousin Virginia's in Riverside."

Lydia left her finger in the journal to mark her place and glanced around the parlor. Her mother had never mentioned any of this. Lydia only met her grandparents once before they passed away, and her Uncle Charles and his wife kept to themselves at their farm north of Good Springs. As a child, she had never wondered why they didn't gather for special occasions. It had seemed normal for grown-ups to have their own families. So why did it bother her so much now that her siblings wanted to establish their own holiday traditions too?

Andrew rolled onto his side and started chewing on a rag toy. Lydia rubbed the baby's back with one hand and reopened the journal with the other.

My parents stayed up on the wagon bench when they dropped me off at the Colburns' house on their way out of Good Springs. I kissed them both and took Mr. Colburn's hand as I stepped down. He was an august older man with a soothing voice, which is pleasant in an overseer considering how the church must listen to his sermons each week.

Mrs. Colburn hoisted a basket of food up to my parents for their journey. They hardly gave it a glance. Mrs. Colburn wiped her hands on her apron as she kindly wished them well.

The whole day had been shrouded in a dreamlike haze. I hadn't thought about John Colburn being there until he lifted my trunk from the back of the wagon. John was the Colburns' eldest son and only living child. Seven years my senior, he had finished secondary school before I entered, so I didn't know him well. All I knew was that he was polite and serious and would one day inherit his father's property and become overseer of Good Springs.

As John carried my trunk into the house and Mr. Colburn spoke with my parents, Mrs. Colburn walked me toward the back door. She chirped about baking and Christmas decorations and all the amusing things we could do during my stay. Her cheerful demeanor was like a ray of sunlight peeking between storm clouds. I couldn't take my eyes off her.

Once inside the Colburns' warm kitchen, I heard my parents' wagon drive away. I stepped to the window to wave, but they were already gone.

"There now," Mrs. Colburn cooed as she ushered me away from the window, "this will all be for the best. You'll see."

Chapter Eight

Lydia drew her pen from its silver holder beside the lamp on her desk and dipped it in the ink well. She pressed the pen to a fresh piece of gray leaf paper and marked a straight line an inch from the top. "I always start a fresh chart for each new patient. According to my mentor," she glanced at Sophia, "your grandfather, Doctor Ashton, some patients' information will barely fill one chart in their entire lifetimes, and other patients will need— or want—medical attention so often their records will overflow a file."

Sophia asked, "Do you use ink for all of your notes?"

"No, only for the name and personal details. I use pencil for my observations and treatment notes. I've never had an assistant before, but until you are knowledgeable in medical terms, I want you to report your observations to me and

I'll note the patient charts. I file the charts in here," she said as she opened the drawer at the right side of her desk, "by the patient's last name."

Sophia pointed to the drawer at Lydia's left. "What's in there?"

Lydia hadn't told her father about the journal yet, so she certainly didn't intend to tell anyone else. "That drawer is… hard to open. Leave it alone." She smoothed her hair and stood from her desk. "I'll show you where we'll conduct our research with the gray leaf."

Sunlight filtered into Lydia's office through the gauzy curtains and lit Sophia's young smile. She clasped her creamy white hands. "This is what I've been waiting for!"

"I'm glad you're excited about research," Lydia said as she led her to the long counter between a bookcase and the patient cot. "I used to be the same way, and I hope to regain the fervor that used to keep me at the microscope for hours."

"Used to? What changed?"

"Life!" A laugh escaped Lydia's throat. "I got married and had a baby and my aunt needed more care and… I'm hoping your enthusiasm is infectious." She moved her medical instruments to the cabinet above the counter and set out her microscope, slides, and samples from the gray leaf tree. "Have you used a microscope before?"

Sophia shook her head. "We didn't have one at my school in Woodland. And when I arrived in Good Springs, Mr. Bradshaw said the class had already finished their biology lessons for the year."

"Not to worry, you'll get plenty of practice here. First, I'll show you how to prepare a slide." She picked up two slides, handed Sophia one of the thin pieces of glass, and began to demonstrate. "Lay the slide flat like this." She pointed at the samples. "These gray leaves are at various stages in their development. We only want one layer of the leaf. If it's too thick, we won't be able to see the cells."

She sliced a section of a fresh gray leaf with a scalpel, and its scent filled the air. She inhaled deeply as she peeled the top layers of the leaf apart with tweezers. "Now we place our leaf sample on the slide," she picked up a water dropper, "and then we drip a small amount of—"

A knock on the office door interrupted her demonstration. She set the dropper on the counter, crossed the office floor, and opened the door. "Oh hello, Nicholas. Come in."

"Thank you, Dr. Bradshaw." He removed his hat as he stepped inside. His hair was freshly washed and his clothes clean and pressed. The smell of soap clung to the air around him. He didn't look like a farmhand who had stopped in the middle of his day to run an errand in the village. "I've come to return your—" His words were cut short as his gaze landed on Sophia.

Lydia's new assistant was peering through the microscope's eyepiece, waving a finger across the stage and watching it pass the lenses. She had yet to give Nicholas a glance, and it was a pity she was missing his open-jawed stare of wonder as he took in her young female form.

Lydia rolled her eyes at Nicholas. "Coming to return my what?"

He peeled his gaze away from Sophia. "Your jar." He held out the empty salve container she had sent home with him a week prior.

"That's very kind of you, but it wasn't necessary. How is your foot?"

His worshiping eyes had wandered back to Sophia. "My what?"

"The nail puncture on the bottom of your foot? The wound that required the salve that was in this jar, which you are so kindly and unnecessarily returning?"

"Quite well, thank you," he said without glancing at Lydia.

She touched his arm and regained his attention. "Shall I introduce you?"

"Hm?"

"To my new assistant?"

"Yes, please do." Nicholas lowered his voice. "We met long ago. She might not remember me, but I'd like to say hello. Everett told me she was training here now with you. He thought it might be a good time for me to return your jar."

"I'll bet he did."

"Pardon?"

"Never mind." She grinned and led him toward the counter. "Sophia, I'd like to introduce you to—"

The instant Sophia turned to look, her smile lit the room. "Nicholas Vestal?"

Lydia glanced between them. "Ah, see there, Nicholas, she does remember you."

Sophia beamed. "Of course, I do. Nicholas is from Woodland too. I haven't seen you since we were children. Well, I was a child anyway." She glanced at Lydia briefly. "When I was in primary school, Nicholas was finishing high school. You were a year ahead of my sister, Alice, weren't you?"

"Two years actually. I believe... um, yes, two years." Nicholas's fingers had a slight tremble that vibrated the brim of the hat he held. It was a good thing Sophia was comfortable making conversation.

"Alice and her family have been in Good Springs for three years now. I've been here since July."

"Since July? I've been here since my aunt sent word to me that the Fosters needed a farmhand over a year ago." Nicholas fidgeted with his hat. "I'm working to get my own flock and possibly some land here."

"Oh, how lovely."

Lydia leaned against her desk as she watched the awkward exchange. The young man was clearly infatuated with Sophia and probably had been coached by Everett and the other shepherds to come and talk to her. Lydia wanted to let it play out, but it would only encourage future interruptions of their work if she didn't act now. She stepped to the door. "Nicholas, thank you for so kindly returning the jar. Most people don't think of such things. It was very thoughtful. Sophia and I were about to begin some research, though, and we need to get back to work."

"Yes, well, I should be going." He threaded the brim of his hat through his fingers as he backed toward the door. "Thank you again, Doctor, for your excellent care. And Sophia, it was a pleasure meeting you again… here… seeing you here in Good Springs… where we both live now… all grown up." His foot tapped the threshold and he waved goodbye with his hat instead of his hand. "See you around."

Sophia's smile held steady and she gave a feminine wave. "See you around, Nicholas."

Lydia restrained her groan as she closed the door. She was never that young. And she certainly didn't remember Connor being that dopey when he was first in love with her. Nicholas was a nice enough fellow, handsome even, but Lydia had the overwhelming urge to screen her trainee's potential suitors. "He's intrigued with you."

"Yes, I realized that." Sophia had already returned her attention to the microscope. "How do you adjust these lenses?"

Lydia reached for one of the dials and turned it as Sophia looked through. "It's not my business really if you plan to court anyone, but I assumed since you want to train with me, your work would be your priority. Not that you aren't allowed to court while you're in training… I just didn't consider it before I brought you on."

"Would it have made a difference to you?"

Lydia shrugged. "It will make a difference in how accustomed I allow myself to get with having you around."

"What do you mean?"

"If you fall in love and get married and have babies, that would likely end your work here, wouldn't it?"

Sophia let go of the microscope. "I hadn't thought of that. I hope to get married someday and when I do… yes, I want to make a home of my own. I'm not sure how much work I'd be able to do while having a family to take care of." She furrowed her brow. "How did you plan your life that it works so well for you?"

"Oh, I didn't plan it like it is," Lydia laughed. "All I wanted was to be a doctor and care for the village and explore all the medicinal potential of the gray leaf tree. There is only one bedroom upstairs because I was quite adamant that I would not marry and have children. But when Connor came along, everything changed for me. He assured me that it was possible for me to continue my work and raise a family."

"Was he right? Is it possible?"

Lydia glanced out the window at the Colburn house. Her son was in there napping while Bethany babysat him. Her father was behind the chicken coop, taking care of their dinner. "It has been possible so far, but I've had my family's help."

Sophia picked up a sample of the gray leaf. "I haven't been in Good Springs very long, but from what I know of your family, it seems like they would make anything possible."

Lydia wasn't so sure anymore. Bethany would soon marry and move away, her other siblings no longer wanted to come home for Christmas, and her father was getting older. Could she still count on her family?

She wanted to talk to someone about the way she felt, but not her young trainee. Mandy was her best friend, but as Levi's wife she was now extended family and part of the problem. Aunt Isabella had been her confidant when fear and doubt crept in, but she was gone now. Maybe that was why Isabella gave her the little journal—as one final word of encouragement written by the only person Lydia always trusted: her mother.

Chapter Nine

At midnight Lydia crawled into bed, weary from a long day. Raindrops hit the window with an arrhythmic tink tink tink that made her wish it would either commit to downpour or stop altogether. Instead of putting out her lamp, she slid it close to the edge of her bedside table and opened her mother's journal. So far, the sadness of her mother's predicament had only reinforced her own. Still, she yearned to read another page of the story.

Mrs. Colburn handed me a beige apron that had a pink rose embroidered on the collar. She said it was mine to keep and insisted I call her Violet when the men weren't around. She was always busy in the house or the garden or the kitchen and kept me with her from chore to chore.

I liked the work. She had a tip or trick to make everything easier or better. At first I thought she was inventing projects to keep me occupied so that I'd forget about my troubles, but she wasn't. She did everything out of genuine love for her family and her home.

Two days before Christmas, she started preparing the food. She said she made the same feast every year, even when it would be only Mr. Colburn, John, and Mr. Colburn's blind sister, Isabella, and herself at the dinner table. It seemed extravagant to spend two days cooking for four people, but she said as the overseer's wife, she never knew who else might join them and she wanted to be prepared. Some Christmases travelers needed hospitality, and some Christmases people were alone and she invited them over. Since I fit into both of those categories, I smiled and continued pitting cherries for the salad recipe she was teaching me.

Isabella sat at the table, snapping green beans. She had a funny way of being so quiet for so long, I'd forget she was around, and then she'd interject some comment proving she listened to every word spoken in the Colburn house.

As I worked on the cherries, Violet made the sauce at the cook stove. "Beat two eggs in your saucepan with a wooden spoon like so, and then add one cup of sugar and one cup of heavy whipping cream." She scraped every drip of cream out of the cup. "The trick is to keep stirring the sauce on medium heat for about fifteen minutes. For the perfect cherry salad, you'll want the sauce thick, but be careful not to burn it."

My fingers were tired by the time I'd finished pitting thirty ounces of cherries, but the smell of the warm sweet sauce assured me the work would be worth it. I carried the bowl of cherries to Violet. "When do we mix these into the sauce?"

She wagged a finger at me and moved the saucepan from the cook stove to a potholder on the countertop. "Oh, not for hours. We have to let the sauce and the cherries chill before we mix them together. And we'll mix in a cup of crushed walnuts then too. Now, keep those cherries in their juices and cover the bowl. I want you to take it down to the cellar to chill in the icebox. Then come back for this sauce. I'll have it in a covered dish by then."

I held the bowl of cherries with both hands as I stepped out the back door and descended the sunny steps to the dark cellar. As I pushed the heavy wooden door open and stared into the blackness inside, I was overcome with grief. I'd spent the day cooking with Violet in her warm sunlit kitchen and had enjoyed it so very much that I'd forgotten the dark loneliness that awaited me.

I leaned against the open door without a ray of light touching me and closed my eyes. My tears fell silently at first, but were swiftly followed by forceful weeping. Bereft, I forgot all about the cherries and cried.

I don't know if I heard him coming, but when I think back, I know I felt him there. At once, the bowl was taken from me and a hand was on my shoulder. I wiped away the tears that blurred my vision. John Colburn was standing there, holding the bowl and looking down at me. His steel blue eyes were full of concern. I hid my face in my hands. "I'm so sorry you saw me like this. Please go."

I heard movement and peeked between my fingers, hoping he'd left the cellar. Instead, he set the bowl in the icebox and lit a lantern. He blew out the match and turned back to me. "You need light."

"Thank you." Ashamed he could now clearly see my face, I tried to blink back my tears. "I didn't come down here to cry."

"I know."

"It's just that your mother is so kind and your house is so peaceful and until I came down here I'd forgotten I have to leave in a few days and not just leave this house but the village. My home. This village is my home. I am a grown woman and my parents said I had to go with them to Northpoint or go to my cousin's in Riverside, but I don't want to. I want to stay here in Good Springs, but my brother's wife didn't want me to live with them. My father said I'm still his responsibility since I'm unmarried, but the best he could come up with was to send me away. But I don't want to leave Good Springs."

I stepped toward John and he wrapped me in his arms, reflexively, which was fitting because he was training to be the overseer and I would not be the last sobbing person he would have to console. He didn't say a word. He let me bury my face against him and cry. I was so absorbed in my self-pity I didn't think anything of his kindness until I had cried all I could. And then I pulled away.

He towered over me and smelled like sunshine and the gray leaf trees. I had always thought of him as older and dignified, in an unapproachable scholarly sort of way. But he wasn't. He didn't stop me as I backed away and he wouldn't have stopped me if I had dropped into his arms and wept again. His unmovable compassion stunned me.

I didn't mean for it to happen, nor did I see it coming, but that was the moment I fell in love with John Colburn.

Chapter Ten

Late in the afternoon on Christmas Day, I helped Violet set the table. She had a place for every dish on the buffet and a purpose for every decoration. Even the wreath on the outside of the kitchen door was to let passersby know they were welcome to come and share the feast.

Once the roast was carved, I hung my apron beside hers on the pantry door and hoped I would remember to pack it later. I tried not to think about having to leave the next day as I watched the family gather in the spacious kitchen.

Isabella tapped her cane as she walked in from the parlor. She felt for her seat at the end of the table and opened her napkin with a snap. Mr. Colburn pulled out Violet's chair for her, and then he moved to the head of the table. John sat at Mr. Colburn's left, across from

Violet. There was an empty seat beside him and also one on the opposite side next to Violet.

I stayed by the pantry door and dithered a moment, unsure about where to sit. My heart longed to be near John, but it was foolish since I had to leave town the next day. I watched Violet for my cue, but she didn't look back at me. I smoothed my lavender calico dress and straightened Mother's silver turtle-shaped brooch over my top button. Mr. Colburn noticed me and cleared his throat. John stood and pulled the chair out beside him. "I am sorry, Hannah. Please, sit here."

Surrounded by a caring family, with the stone hearth behind me and a bountiful feast covering the table before me, my heart swelled with love. Their abundant hospitality bandaged my wounded soul. Even if I never saw the Colburn family again, I would cherish that feeling in my heart and draw upon its warmth for the rest of my life.

Mr. Colburn bowed his head to say the blessing. I closed my eyes and folded my hands like we did at church, but John took my hand in his. I flinched and opened my eyes. They had all joined hands. Violet gave me a wink and Isabella felt along the table for my other hand.

Mr. Colburn thanked God for sending His Son into the world and asked God to keep the purpose of Christmas at the center of the village families' celebrations. I tried to focus on Mr. Colburn's words as he prayed, but all I could think about was John's hand holding mine. It was silly to think he meant any more by taking my hand than Isabella did, but his hand enveloped mine with a dominant firmness. When Mr. Colburn said 'Amen,' John didn't immediately let go.

Later that evening, I shook out the apron Violet had given me and took it to the guestroom to pack in the musty trunk from my parents' house. I sat on the edge of the bed and traced my fingers along the seams of its soft quilt. I didn't want to move to Riverside, but there were no other options. I sighed and stood to pack, but my trunk wasn't in the room.

It must have stunk too much for Violet to keep in her house. She'd mentioned setting it out in the sun the day I arrived, but I'd forgotten all about it. I left the guestroom to go search for it outside.

As I passed Isabella's bedroom, I peeked in. She was sitting in the dark in a rocking chair by the draped window, knitting. "John has it in the barn," she called out to me.

"Pardon?"

"If you're looking for your trunk, John has it in the barn."

"Why?"

Isabella's knitting needles clicked rhythmically. "I can't speak for him, child. Go out there and ask him yourself."

Dusk darkened the yard, and crickets sang into the cool evening breeze. I ambled through the grass toward the barn, wishing I could make my time with the Colburns last longer. One barn door was propped open, and a faint swishy-scratching sound came from inside.

"Hello?" I called from the doorway. A lantern's soft glow filled the open space in the center of the barn. John was kneeling in front of my trunk, holding a sanding block.

"In here," he answered. "Mother had your trunk sitting in the sun all week, but it was still musty, so I am sanding the inside of it."

"That's very thoughtful. Thank you."

"I wanted to have it done before you were finished helping her with the dishes. I am sorry it is taking so long."

He might have meant for me to go back to the house, but I didn't want to. I glanced around the barn. A dark horse with a white blaze was peering over one of the stall gates. "Do you mind if I wait here?"

John shook his head. He tossed the sanding block onto a workbench and pulled a rag from his back pocket. As he cleaned the dust out of the freshly sanded trunk, I walked toward the horse.

The smell of fresh hay hung in the air and reminded me of my brother. "Charles always works in the barn in the evenings. He's probably out working in our barn right now. Only it's not our barn anymore—it's his." I glanced back at John. "And his wife's. She hates me. That's why I couldn't stay at home. She doesn't like anyone and wanted the house to herself as soon as they were married."

"Hannah, do not give bitterness a chance to take root." His hands stopped their work and he gave me a look of compassion mixed with authority. "This situation is difficult for you, but God is not surprised by your circumstances."

I moved away from the stalls and stepped toward the lantern on his workbench. "You're right, of course. It all happened so quickly. I'm done crying for my loss, but now I'm dreading the journey ahead. I've never traveled far. Have you been to Riverside?"

John nodded. "Once."

"Was it nice?"

He nodded again and continued cleaning the trunk. I would have offered to help him, but I wanted it to take as long as possible so we could keep talking. He was disinclined to make conversation, but I was determined to hear his voice. "How many days was your journey with the traders when you went to Riverside?"

"I did not ride with a trader."

"Did you take your parents' wagon?"

"No. I traveled by horseback."

"How long did it take?"

He shook the dust from his rag and resumed wiping the trunk. "It is a three-day journey, but it took me longer because I did not go directly to Riverside."

"Why not?"

"It was during my overseer training, so I had to stop at other villages too."

"Was that the trip where you were supposed to find a wife?"

He raised an eyebrow.

"I'm sorry. That came out wrong. I remembered people in the village talking about your visiting all of the other villages in the Land. People thought you would come back married. I'm sorry."

"It is all right, Hannah." A faint smile curved his lips. "When a man is training to be overseer, he must visit the overseers in each village. And yes, if he is unwed, it is often when he finds a wife."

I hadn't thought of it before, but it was possible he could be courting someone or engaged. "Did you… find someone?"

"No. It was not in God's timing."

I was relieved to hear it even though I was to leave the village in a matter of hours. "My parents are hoping I will make a match in Riverside."

"Is that what you want?"

I shrugged. "I want to get married someday, but I always imagined it would be here. I guess it's like you said: God is not surprised by my circumstances." I tried to think of something positive about what I might face. "Maybe God has planned all along for me to move there and take care of my cousin's children. I always hoped He would entrust me with a child's heart and Cousin Virginia has nine kids, so there will be plenty of little hearts for me to love. That's all I really want."

John stopped working and gazed at me for a long moment. I wasn't sure if I had said something he didn't like or something he did. He kept his thoughts to himself and his eyes on me. Finally he gave the trunk one last wipe. Then he dropped the rag and brushed his hands together. "Would you like to see if this is better?"

"If what is better?"

He grinned and pointed at the trunk. "The trunk."

"Oh," I laughed. "I'm sure it's fine. Thank you, again. You didn't have to do it for me."

"I wanted to do something for you. You are a lovely woman. I am sorry for the circumstances that brought you to our home, but I have enjoyed your company."

"Thank you." Hot tears welled up, but I refused to let them fall. No one had ever spoken to me so sweetly. He was kind and thoughtful and wanted better for me than a smelly trunk and a wagon ride to another village. But I was certain I would never see him again, so I excused myself and ran back to the house.

Chapter Eleven

The day after Christmas, I thanked Mr. and Mrs. Colburn for their hospitality. I had never experienced anything like it and told them so. I glanced around their warm kitchen, wishing I could stay there. The aroma of all the Christmas cooking still hung in the air. I took a deep breath of it, but as soon as I stepped outside, I could only smell the nearby ocean.

While John loaded my trunk onto the back of their wagon, Mr. Colburn put his hand on my shoulder and prayed for me. I expected him to ask God to keep me safe as I traveled or something along that line, but instead he prayed that I would delight myself in the Lord and God would give me the desires of my heart. When he was finished, Mrs. Colburn hugged me as if I were her child, and for a moment I felt like I was.

John didn't speak as he drove me to the chapel where I was to wait for the trader. It didn't bother me, though, because I had grown fond of sitting in silence with him. His presence alone was comforting. He was a man of few words. When he chose to speak, he made sure his words mattered. He had my complete respect.

A low fog had settled across the village during the night, and the morning sunlight had yet to burn it off. I gave each house and building we passed a long stare, trying to commit them all to memory—the stone library, the sandy lot where the market was held each week, Doctor Ashton's house, and the beautiful white chapel with its high steeple, stone steps, and black iron railing. I wanted to go inside each building one last time, only I didn't want it to be my last time. I wanted to stay in Good Springs, and all at once I knew that I should. I just didn't know why or how.

John pulled the wagon to the side of the road in front of the chapel. He offered his hand as I stepped down. I took it, thinking he was only being polite, but when I reached the ground he didn't let go. He left my trunk in the wagon and—without a word—walked me to the chapel's stone steps.

When he finally released my hand, he looked down at me. His eyes were filled with kindness. "Surely there is someone in Good Springs."

"Someone?"

"Someone you could live with for a while. A friend perhaps?"

"I don't know of anyone with a spare bed. I went to say goodbye to my friend Roseanna on Tuesday and almost asked her parents if I could stay there, but they already have a house full."

John cast his gaze around the village. There wasn't a soul in sight. He blew out a breath. "If you tell my father how badly you want to stay here, he will send word to your cousin in Riverside."

"I don't want to be a burden."

"We can find a livelihood for you here. Surely someone needs help with children, or maybe you could assist the teacher at the primary school."

"My father told me to go to Riverside."

"I do not want you to leave."

My breath caught. I'm not sure when I let it out or if I ever did. His eyes widened as if he had shocked himself as much as he had shocked me. He took my fingertips in his hands and fixed his gaze on me for one exquisite moment. "Hannah, I have never met a woman like you, nor am I likely to again."

Hoofbeats clip-clopped on the cobblestone street as the trader's wagon rolled into the village, but we both ignored it. The fog began to lift.

John glanced at my hand in his. "I am in love with you. Please do not leave. By tradition, I cannot propose marriage without speaking to your father first, but if you are at all willing to consider me, stay here. I will follow your parents to Northpoint at once and speak to your father. I believe God has brought you into my life. If you feel the same, please stay."

I have been Mrs. John Colburn for over five years now. John and I just had our third child—a little girl we named Lydia. That was Violet's middle name. I've missed her and Mr. Colburn very much since they passed away. It was Violet's hospitality that changed my life and opened my heart on my first Christmas with the Colburns.

I've continued her tradition of preparing a feast on Christmas Day for my family and also for anyone who might need the hospitality. John and I now have three daughters, so I don't know if the next overseer of Good Springs will be a Colburn, but whoever it is, I pray he too will stay prepared to extend hospitality, especially at Christmastime.

A strange and wearisome sadness settled over me after Lydia's birth. Doctor Ashton says it's a common experience for women. I've only told

Isabella, and she gave me this little notebook and told me to write about the happiest time in my life thus far. I didn't like the idea at first, but she said writing this story would help me through my sadness. She was right. Thank you, Isabella.

Chapter Twelve

Orange rays of morning sunlight spilled into the kitchen's east window as Lydia prepared the last recipes for Christmas dinner. John was in the barn milking the cow, and Bethany had already left to spend the day with Everett at the Fosters' farm. It was the first time Lydia had ever known the Colburn house to feel empty on a Christmas morning.

She wiped the sugar and cornstarch from her hands as she checked her mother's lemon pudding recipe once more. While she poured milk into a saucepan, baby Andrew yanked on her apron's hem, trying to stand. She knelt and offered her fingers to help him up.

Babbling, he gripped her thumbs and pulled himself up. His knees buckled and straightened again as he tried to balance. Then he let go of her and took one wobbly step by himself.

"Good boy!" Lydia barely got the words out when he plopped down on the floor again. Though she continued to encourage him, he promptly returned his attention to the slobbery measuring cups he had been playing with. She smoothed his fine hair. "When your father gets home today, he will be delighted to see what you've learned."

She stood and glanced at the road, eager for Connor's return and also watching for any travelers. It might be the quietest Christmas ever in the Colburn house, but that didn't matter anymore. Reading her mother's story had ignited her desire to continue the tradition of being prepared to offer hospitality to others.

John opened the back door and sniffed the air as he set a full milk pail by the sink. "Mmm, do I smell oyster dressing like your mother used to make?"

"You do." Lydia pointed at a stack of faded papers on the counter. "I dug out some of her favorite recipes. We're having roast turkey with oyster dressing, mashed potatoes, turnips, stewed beets, squash, lemon pudding, and Grandmother Colburn's cherry salad."

"Sounds wonderful. I hope Connor makes it home by dinner time." John patted her back and then held out his hands to Andrew as the baby crawled to him. "There is my happy grandson." After a moment with the baby, he rubbed Andrew's head, messing the strands Lydia had just smoothed.

She smiled at them both and began whisking egg yolks for the pudding. John moved about the kitchen, working around her, as Andrew sat on the floor alternating between biting and banging the measuring cups. He glanced at her, and his eyes reminded her of Connor.

She added lemon zest and salt to the saucepan and moved it to the stove to cook. While the pudding warmed, she reached into her dress pocket and pulled out the little journal. "Father, I have something to give you."

John stood at the sink, straining the milk. He didn't look at her. "Not a Christmas present, I hope. I know some of the villagers have started exchanging gifts, but I believe it could lead to a view of Christmas that takes our focus off the Lord."

She and Connor held a different opinion of Christmas presents from that of her father, but they respected him enough to keep their gift exchanging private. "No, Father, it's not a Christmas present."

"Good. I do not want to start any more traditions."

"It's not really from me even, and I probably should have given it to you before I read it." Lydia glanced at her mother's journal. "But it helped me let go of the demands I was placing on everyone because of what I thought Christmas should be."

John furrowed his brow as he dried his fingers with a dishtowel. "What is it?"

She held the notebook out to him. "Aunt Isabella gave it to me before she died. I'm not sure how much she understood during her last few days, but I think she knew I was upset that the others weren't coming here for Christmas dinner. She had this hidden in her wardrobe for years. She wanted me to have it, but it belongs to you."

John accepted the journal and opened it. "This is your mother's handwriting," he whispered.

"It's the story of when she fell in love with you."

Without a word, John walked into the parlor, already reading Hannah's story. He sat in the overstuffed armchair near the hearth and held the pocket-sized book with both hands. Tears welled in the corner of Lydia's eyes as she returned to the stove to stir the pudding.

* * *

Lydia arranged the dishes for Christmas dinner on the buffet near the table and set a warming stone in the center. Andrew wiggled in his high chair, tossing bread cubes to the floor. John stepped to the buffet, holding a steaming pan of carved turkey. He centered the pan on the warmer then removed his oven mitts. "This looks incredible, Lydia. Your mother would be proud of you."

Outside the kitchen window, a dust cloud rose at the end of the property. Lydia yanked off her apron and tossed it onto the counter. "He's here!" She lifted Andrew from his highchair and dashed outside with him.

Connor dismounted and jogged across the yard to meet her. She held the baby and hurried toward Connor. Whiskers darkened his unshaven face, but they didn't dim his charisma. When he reached her, she opened her mouth to say Merry Christmas, but before she could speak, he kissed her.

Andrew squealed and reached for his father. Connor took the baby with one arm and drew Lydia closer with the other. "That was a much better welcome than the first time I came here."

Lydia tucked her hair behind her ear. "Thank God you came back to us in one piece!"

"Just like I said I would. Am I too late for dinner?"

"We haven't eaten yet."

Connor pointed at the medical cottage. "Is Sophia eating with us?"

"No, she went to her sister's house for the day."

"Are you expecting anyone else?"

"No, we were just waiting for you."

Connor inclined his head toward her. "Are you okay?"

"I am." She smiled out of true joy. "I have a lot to tell you about."

A wagon turned onto the property. The man and woman on the bench seat waved, while three children in the wagon bed talked excitedly to each other and pointed at the house. Lydia pulled away from Connor. "Who are they?"

"The Vestal family. I met them on the road. They're traveling to Stonehill this week, and I suggested they stop here for the night. I didn't think you would mind," he grinned at Lydia, "seeing as how you're going to be the next overseer's wife."

"I will be? It's certain then? You decided to train for Father's position?"

"I did." His confidence was softened with humility. "I have a lot to tell you later, too."

Overcome with delight, she didn't know if she should kiss him or greet the guests first. "This is wonderful!"

Connor waved the visitors toward the house and passed the baby back to Lydia. "And there's more."

"More?"

He stepped around his horse, removed something from a strap, and held it up. "The overseer of Woodland sent a wreath for you."

"How beautiful!"

"And Adeline and Maggie sent a few things to make your Christmas a little brighter." He opened one of the saddlebags and reached inside then pulled out several packages one at a time. "Adeline sent cookies and a block of cheese and," he shook a brown paper packet, "these are roasted nuts from Maggie. She and Thomas are expecting their next child. That is why she didn't feel like making the trip today. And Adeline and Isaac wanted to stay in Woodland with them."

"Oh," Lydia said as she took one of the packages. "Now I understand. I wish she'd said that in her letter. Are they all doing well?"

"Yep." Connor glanced over her toward the kitchen door. "Merry Christmas, John!"

"Merry Christmas," John replied. He walked outside and opened his arms to Connor. "Welcome back, son!"

"Thank you, sir. Your daughters sent gifts from Woodland." Connor handed the packages to John and immediately drew another from the saddlebag. "I think this one is fruitcake—everybody's favorite." He winked at Lydia.

The visitors parked their wagon near the house. John took the packages from Connor and said, "I see you have brought guests. Welcome, friends!"

After Connor made introductions, Lydia welcomed the travelers inside to share her feast and her home. She would continue the tradition of hospitality and bless others the way her mother and grandmother had. With a heart full of gratitude for her family—those with her, those absent, and those now with the Lord— she blinked back happy tears. She put Andrew in his high chair and, as the guests washed for dinner, she hung the wreath on the door.

"Looks great," Connor said, smiling.

"Thank you." Lydia paused before stepping back in the full kitchen. She gazed up into the clear blue sky and whispered, "Thank you."

GRANDMA'S CHERRY SALAD RECIPE

2 eggs

1 cup sugar

1 cup heavy whipping cream

(2) 14.5 ounce cans pitted tart red cherries

1 cup crushed walnuts

In a saucepan, beat eggs with a wooden spoon. Add sugar and cream. Cook over medium heat until thick (about 15 minutes), stirring continually as not to burn it. Transfer to a food container and cover. Chill the sauce overnight. Chill the cans of cherries also. Once sauce and cherries are cold, drain cherries. In a 2-quart bowl, pour sauce over well-drained cherries and add crushed walnuts. Toss salad gently and chill until ready to serve.

Author's note:

This recipe was handed down to my mother from her grandmother. We don't know how many generations it has been in the family, but we enjoy it with every holiday meal. I hope you do too!

More Books by Keely Brooke Keith

The Land Uncharted (#1)

Lydia Colburn is a young physician dedicated to serving her village in the Land, an undetectable island in the South Atlantic Ocean. When Lt. Connor Bradshaw's parachute carries him from the war engulfing the 2025 world to Lydia's hidden land, his mission could expose her simple society. As Connor searches for a way to return to his squadron, his fascination with life in the Land makes him protective of Lydia and her peaceful homeland, and Lydia's attraction to Connor stirs desires she never anticipated. But will they be able to keep the Land hidden?

Uncharted Redemption (#2)

Spirited violinist Mandy Foster spends her days building musical instruments and her nights regretting her past. If anyone discovers her secret, tradition dictates the village will shun her. She guards her heart with skillfully played songs and flirtatious smiles.

Breaking from the Land's tradition, carpenter Levi Colburn is building his house outside the village—across the road from Mandy to be exact. Though he longs to marry Mandy, she rejected him once and has been unattainable to every man in the village ever since.

When rebels tear through Good Springs and abduct Mandy, it's up to Levi to find her. But will she accept the tender care of the one man who truly loves her?

Uncharted Inheritance (#3)

Bethany Colburn is finally allowed to court and Everett Foster is ready to confess his love for her. As the outside world closes in on the Land, a new man arrives in the village of Good Springs. He brings charm Bethany has never encountered and illness the Land has never known. While the medicinal power of the gray leaf tree is put to the test and the Colburn family's strength is stretched thin, Bethany must choose between the love of her life and the intriguing new man. But nothing will matter if the Land is invaded.

Christmas with the Colburns (#4)

It's Christmastime in Good Springs, and Lydia Bradshaw is eager for the light at the end of her year—the Colburn family's big holiday gathering. When she discovers none of her siblings are coming back to the village this year, she believes Christmas will be ruined. As Lydia faces a gloomy holiday in the Colburn house, an unexpected discovery brightens her favorite season. Will it be enough to rekindle the light of Christmas?

Uncharted Hope (#5)

Sophia Ashton's new medical assistant job comes with the perks of living on the Colburn property, which include being surrounded by a loving family—something she's never known. During the job's trial period, a patient puts Sophia in a questionable position. Now she must prove her competence or lose her job and home.

Nicholas Vestal is working on a sheep farm to earn a starter flock, but before his contract is up, he inherits a house in the village. While fixing up the old house, he pursues Sophia Ashton, believing she is the woman God wants him to marry. But when Sophia's difficult past blocks Nicholas's plan, he must find a way to her heart.

Meanwhile, outside the Land...

When plant biologist Bailey Colburn is offered a research job, she knows Justin Mercer is playing her somehow. Working for the former naval flight officer sounds better than her other options in post-war Norfolk, even though Justin says he once met her long lost relatives. But when Justin introduces Bailey to the mysterious gray leaf tree, his unbelievable claims change her world.

Uncharted Journey (#6)

Young widow Eva Vestal assumes loneliness is God's permanent plan for her life. She keeps busy by raising her son and co-managing the

Inn at Falls Creek with her elderly father, but her heart yearns for more.

Solomon "Solo" Cotter has spent his life working with horses, but he secretly wants to write a book of the children's stories his grandfather told him as a boy. He barters with Eva's father for a 40-night stay at the inn, a needed respite from work to get his stories on paper.

Once Eva discovers the barter, she believes Solo is taking advantage of her father's failing memory. But when tragedy strikes and Solo works hard to save the inn, Eva sees his true nature. As her heart stirs with feelings for Solo, she wrestles with the guilt of loving someone new.

Meanwhile, outside the Land...

Bailey Colburn arrives at the coordinates of the Land on the autumn equinox and finds nothing but ocean. The sun sets, ending Bailey's dream of a safe and simple life with the family she's never known. Just when she decides Justin Mercer lied about visiting a hidden land in the South Atlantic Ocean and meeting Bailey's distant relatives, the atmosphere around the boat changes and ushers her into an uncharted world, but her entrance into the Land comes at a devastating price.

Uncharted Destiny (#7)

Bailey Colburn is safe in the Land, but her father figure, Professor Tim, never made it to Good Springs. When Bailey discovers Tim is lost in the Land's dangerous mountain terrain and out of his life-saving medication, she sets out to rescue him. Even with the help of intriguing native Revel Roberts, Bailey faces an impossible journey to save Tim. The mountains are shrouded in dark folklore and full of deadly surprises.

Revel Roberts never stays in one place too long. No matter where he travels in the Land, he avoids the Inn at Falls Creek, his boyhood home and the business he will inherit. But when fearless newcomer Bailey Colburn needs Revel's help to find her friend, he joins the mission and is forced to return to the place he'd rather forget.

Bailey and Revel's friendship strengthens as they need each other in ways neither of them imagined. But nothing can prepare them for what awaits in the Land's treacherous mountains.

Visit www.keelybrookekeith.com for more details.

About Keely Brooke Keith

Keely Brooke Keith writes inspirational frontier-style fiction with a futuristic twist, including *The Land Uncharted* (Shelf Unbound Notable Romance 2015) and *Aboard Providence* (2017 INSPY Awards Longlist).

Born in St. Joseph, Missouri, Keely was a tree-climbing, baseball-loving 80s kid. She grew up in a family who moved often, which fueled her dreams of faraway lands. When she isn't writing, Keely enjoys teaching home school lessons and playing bass guitar. Keely, her husband, and their daughter live on a hilltop south of Nashville, Tennessee.

Made in the USA
Coppell, TX
13 December 2019